SHADY BABY

Written by
GABRIELLE UNION-WADE
and DWYANE WADE JR.

Inspired by
KAAVIA JAMES UNION-WADE

Illustrated by
TARA NICOLE WHITAKER

HARPER
An Imprint of HarperCollinsPublishers

Shady Baby • Copyright © 2021 by Kaavia James, Inc. • All rights reserved. Printed in the United States of America. No part of this book may be used or reproduced in any manner whatsoever without written permission except in the case of brief quotations embodied in critical articles and reviews. • For information address HarperCollins Children's Books, a division of HarperCollins Publishers, 195 Broadway, New York, NY 10007. • www.harpercollinschildrens.com ISBN 978-0-06-305403-5 • The artist used Photoshop to create the digital illustrations for this book. Typography by Chelsea C. Donaldson • 21 22 23 24 25 PC 10 9 8 7 6 5 4 3 2 1 ❖ First Edition

Yου are about to meet our girl, Shady Baby.

Now, everyone has an idea of who she is, but do they *really* know?

As you read her story, we hope that you enjoy how Shady Baby gently leads others, uses her voice, remains direct and clear, and holds her peers accountable. Her shade manifests as a look, comment, or gesture, but—however she expresses it—shade is also her superpower. It's a specific way that she, and all children, can shape a better world . . . one side-eye at a time. And if anyone knows how to master shade, it's Shady Baby.

We can't wait for you all to meet her (so go ahead, turn the page).

Love,
Gabrielle and Dwyane

This is Shady Baby!

She's cute but keeps it real.
Shady might be tiny,
but she's a mighty big deal!

Shady shakes things up
as she conquers every day.
'Cause Shady gets things done
in her Shady Baby way . . .

How's Shady Baby feeling?
She always lets it show!

What is Shady thinking?
She will *always* let you know.

Shady raises her eyebrows.

Shady scratches her chin.

You know exactly what's up
when she flashes a grin.

Shady wakes up early,
before the sun shines bright.
Looking this fabulous
won't just happen overnight.

Shady Baby is fly!
She's a trendy tastemaker.
Shirt!
Pants!
Kicks!
She's a fashion-rule breaker.

Shady checks out the mirror.
She turns this and that way.
She's so fresh and so clean—
all set to start her day.

First, Shady hits the pool,
where she splashes, floats, and swims.
At the deck-side party,
Shady grooves while she spins!

No break time for Shady—
the afternoon is still young!

Shady zips down the slide.
The park is always big fun.

Letting trouble happen?!
Shady Baby's not the one!

When others push and shove,
someone has to save the day!
So Shady Baby steps up
in her Shady Baby way!

Shady stands real tall,
flashing her famous side-eye.

Then she says to the girl,
"You should give kindness a try.

"Let me tell you some things
every baby has to learn:
We don't push.
We don't shove.
We wait *nicely* for our turn."

Shady sat in the sand
and broke the cookie in two.
Make things a little sweeter?
That's something she can do.

The Shady Baby Way
makes playtime so much better.
With Shady in the mix,
everyone plays . . . together!

But one girl gets jealous
of how the other kids play.

She sneaks up on Shady,
grabs her toy, and runs away!

When her lip begins trembling
and tears fill up her eyes,

Shady's friends gather around
at the sound of her cries.

Her new friends want to help.
What would Shady Baby do?
They stand up tall, flash a look,
and they say what is true:

"We share with each other
'cause there's always enough.
We don't grab from our friends
or run away with their stuff."

"I'm sorry," the girl says.
"Can I join you all to play?"

Shady thinks it over
in her Shady Baby way. . . .

"Okay." Shady Baby smiles.
"You can join our crew

only if you learn to play
the way that *real* friends do."

Shady Baby takes charge;
she's a leader every day.
And justice will get served hot
when Shady gets a say!

Just call me
tushy, 'cause
I'm wiped!

Sure, her days are busy—
she's a boss who runs the show!
But before Shady rests,
there's one more place to go. . . .

Warm and cozy at home,
Shady Baby snuggles close.
Cuddling with her family
is the thing she loves most.